Jake
the growling dog

For Lyla, Ella, Ava, Mia, and Maci, my family of girls who show
kindness, acceptance, and a love for all of the beautiful differences.
- S.S

For Kathryn and Kamryn, my two beautifully unique rays of
sunshine who have never met a dog or a critter who they do not love.
May you always be as good as you are now at finding the beauty
in the world around you, and may you always love what makes you "you".
- K.J.

Jake the Growling Dog
Copyright © 2019 by Samantha Shannon & Kerrie Joyce
Rawlings Books, LLC

Visit Jake's website at jakethegrowlingdog.com

Book Design by Kerrie Joyce

The characters and events portrayed in this book are fictitious.
Any similarity to real persons, living or dead, is coincidental
and not intended by the author.

Paperback Edition ISBN 978-0-9984053-6-0
Hardback Edition ISBN 978-0-9984053-7-7
Mobi Edition ISBN 978-0-9984053-8-4

Jake
the growling dog

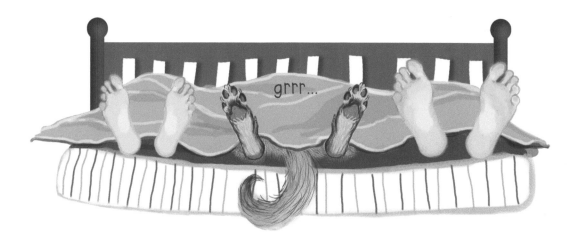

grrr...

Written by Samantha Shannon
Illustrated by Kerrie Joyce

Rawlings Books, LLC

In an emerald-green forest in the Pacific Northwest,
you'll find Jake—a misunderstood dog at best.

He has fur like fresh cotton candy, large pointy ears,
and a big bushy tail that gets puffier each year.

He has a caramel coat, a chocolate stripe down his face,
and each tasty shade is in just the right place.

Jake is fast! Quite fast they say,
with a twitch and a spring as he goes on his way.

Jake loves to run among the tallest of trees,
swim in deep rivers, and chase after Frisbees.
But no matter what Jake loves to do,
you'll always hear him growling, too.

He growls while he **eats,**

grrr...

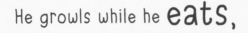

grrr...

He growls while he **plays,**

and he growls while

being **scratched** in

his favorite ear place.

He growls while he sleeps, he growls while he **swims,**

grrr...

and he growls in his bed while being **tucked in.**

grrr...

One day Jake was hiking a trail lined with thistle,
and two yellow warblers flew by with a whistle.

"Why do you growl?" they asked, looking sad.
"What is it that always makes you so mad?"

"I'm not mad," Jake growled cheerfully.
"I'm just as happy as can be."

"I'm having fun out here on the trail,
dashing around and wagging my tail."

"But Jake, don't you notice that animals run away,
and even the little children won't play?"

Jake thought for a moment as he stopped for a sniff,
then he chewed on a perfectly good-looking stick.

He growled while he thought, and with each snapping chew,
his mind wandered back, and it wasn't good news.

He growled at Molly when she scratched his ears.
It was a growl of delight, but she ran off in fear.

grrr...

He growled at the
neighbor's dog every day.

"Hi, Mr. Pomeranian!
Do you want to play?"

But the dog always
left without a goodbye.

Jake assumed that
he was just shy.

Jake didn't know why
everyone was so scared.

How could he show them
how much he cared?

They said it was his
growly voice—could it be?

Did it make him
sound that unfriendly?

While lost in his thoughts, Jake bit down on his lip.
He cried out in pain and whimpered a bit.

Yet to the birds, it was the scariest of growls.
It sounded more like a frightening howl.

Full of fear, they took flight from the trees,
leaving nothing but the falling flutter of leaves.

"Why doesn't anyone understand me?
Why can't they see I'm not actually mean?"

But nobody answered because Jake was alone.
By himself in the forest, all on his own.

grrr...

Then he heard an "eh-hem," a faint whispering call.
Maybe he wasn't alone after all!

"Up here, Jake the Growling Dog. I know,
your growl is your voice. You're just saying hello."

Jake looked around, he looked up, he looked down;
he became quite dizzy spinning around.

Zooming above at spectacular speeds,
a flicker of blackness flew through the trees.

grrr...

It was a lone black squirrel nearly too swift to see.
Jake couldn't find her; she was so fast indeed.

"I like you, Jake. You have a big heart, I can see.
Really that's all that's important to me."

"But others are scared," Jake said with a groan.
"Playing just isn't that fun on my own."

"I'll help you," squeaked the squirrel from the tree.

"We'll work on your growl to make it friendly."

So, Jake and the squirrel, whose name was Neet,
spent days trying to make his voice sound sweet.

Neet begged other animals to help with their training,
but it took plenty of urging, and they just kept complaining.

A painted turtle stayed in her shell for a week
after Neet tried to have the two of them meet.

grrr...

A black-tailed deer was so frightened by him
that she bucked about wildly and started to spin.

Then there was the bufflehead duck that heard Jake.
He let out a "squawk!" and flew out of the lake!

"Oh, what's the use?" cried Jake in despair.
"They don't understand me. They don't even care."

Then something magical happened no one could explain,
as more and more animals watched them each day.

They watched from shadows, ferns, and high perches in trees;
from lakes, from rocks, and trickling streams.

The more they watched, the more they could see,
that Jake was just misunderstood, they agreed.

Jake was kind, he was sweet, though he growled all day.
He was different, they noticed, which was more than okay.

Soon, dogs played with him, and owners and children, too.
They scratched his ears and gave him treats to chew.

They played with him with balls and sticks,
and even taught him cool new tricks.

Jake was happier than he'd ever been,
so he growled the greatest of growls.

One that shook his body and ruffled his fur,
sending off sweet cotton candy smells.

grrr...

But then he stopped short—did he scare his new friends?
He winced and he thought, "Oh no, not again!"

Yet when he opened his eyes, his friends hadn't strayed.
They smiled and laughed, ready to play.

grrr...

The End!

We're all different,
and that's okay.
It makes us unique in
our own special way.

Jake's Loving-Kindness

Each of you can be kind like Neet, Jake, and his new friends by practicing being thankful (gratitude) and through unconditional care, kindness, and love for yourself and others every day with loving-kindness. These wonderful ways of caring for others, the world, and yourself will not only make you and those around you happy, it will also make the world a better place.

Being thankful every day is easy.

For example, you can be thankful for:

- Your fingers, eyes, ears
- Family and friends
- Trees that give you oxygen
- Your dog who loves you unconditionally
- Our men and women in the military who protect us
- The cashier who helped you at the grocery store

- Your teacher for helping you learn to count, read, and write
- Doctors who heal us
- The farmers who grow our vegetables
- The sun for giving us warmth
- And water, for keeping us and our world alive

Practicing loving-kindness is easy as well.

You can show kindness to the new student in your class by introducing yourself, by talking to the girl who looks or talks differently than you, by opening the door for the boy in the wheelchair, and by always thanking others for helping you.

Show yourself love and kindness by thanking yourself for the book you read, the project you finished, the game you played well, the race you ran, how you helped your family today, and for being a good friend, student, brother, sister, daughter, or son.

Being kind to and thankful for yourself is the most important thing for your happiness, and loving yourself is the key to loving and caring for others. It will also help you remember all the incredible things about you when there may be some days that aren't so great, because you are awesome, amazing, outstanding, wonderful, special, and loved.

On the next page is a fun activity you can do with your family to help practice loving-kindness every day! Remember, be kind, thankful, and loving to others, to the world, and most importantly, to yourself.

Jake's Loving-Kindness Activity

This activity is perfect for families to do at home and for schools. Jake recommends doing this each day to help children use loving-kindness for others and themselves. Loving-kindness is a focus on being kind and caring towards ourselves and others.

This practice can lead to overall happiness, joy, acceptance, and gratitude (being thankful). We all have tough days when we feel sad, different, and hurt. This activity is an excellent coping mechanism that allows children to express their feelings and find joy in their day, instead of letting one moment or person ruin it for them. It will also help them feel more connected to the wonders of this world.

Jake has found bedtime to be a fantastic time for this loving-kindness activity. It helps everyone fall asleep happy, which leads to great sleep and awesome mornings!

Step 1:

Get into a comfortable posture, sitting up or lying down.

Step 2:

Send Loving-Kindness to yourself.

Have each person take turns repeating: May I be happy, may I be healthy and strong, may I be peaceful. You can use different words if you like.

Step 3:

Send Loving-Kindness to someone you love or are grateful for.

Give your child time to think of someone on their own before helping.
Have each person take a turn repeating: May (Name) be happy, may (Name) be healthy
and strong, and may (Name) be peaceful.

Step 4:

Send Loving-Kindness to someone you don't know very well.

This person can be a new student in school, neighbor, teacher, or someone they met
at the playground. Have each person take a turn repeating: May (Name) be happy,
may (Name) be healthy and strong, and may (Name) be peaceful.

Step 5:

Send Loving-Kindness to someone you have had difficulty with.

This person can be someone difficult to get along with at school, a friend they had a disagreement
with, or a sibling. It is powerful when a child sees an adult express difficulty with someone. The child
feels like they are not alone - that makes them hopeful. Have each person take a turn repeating: May
(Name) be happy, may (Name) be healthy and strong, and may (Name) be peaceful.

Step 6:

Send Loving-Kindness to every living being in the whole wide world!

Have each person take a turn repeating: May the whole wide world be happy, may the whole wide
world be healthy and strong, and may the whole wide world be peaceful.

Step 7:

Repeat Nightly.

Doing this every night leads to happier children and families.
Enjoy smiles, happiness, and goodnight hugs and kisses!

Thank You and Acknowledgements

We want to thank Dr. Christine Carter and Sharon Salzberg for their teachings on mindfulness and loving-kindness.
Jake's Loving-Kindness Activity is an adaptation of their previously published works.

We also want to acknowledge our muse, Jake the Growling Dog, for his adoring character,
legendary Frisbee and hiking skills, and for being an amazing dog and member of our family.

Jake's Story Continues!

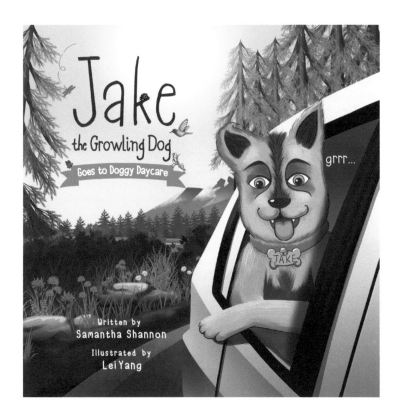

Jake is off to daycare, but he's worried about what's in store.
Going somewhere new can be scary--trying something different, even more.
How will he get ready, and what will help him through?
What will bring him comfort and help prepare him for something new?

Jake the Growling Dog Goes to Doggy Daycare is a book about Trying New Things, Friendship, Finding Comfort, Relieving Stress, and Kindness. Filled with new critters, more social-emotional activities, and a bright, colorful gentle story for families, schools, counseling offices, and more!

Printed in the USA
CPSIA information can be obtained
at www.ICGtesting.com
LVHW071303041123
762975LV00014B/20